YES, YOU CAN!
SAID THE TOUCAN

MARIANA SUAREZ

Illustrations created by: Tanja Tadic

Paperback: 978-1-64085-694-3
Hardback: 978-1-64085-695-0

Library of Congress Control Number: 2019905538

DEDICATION

Thank you to all the wonderful individuals in my life (you know who you are)
for the infinite encouragement, support and for believing in me.
I am forever grateful and hold you all very close to my heart <3
Cheers to new adventures!

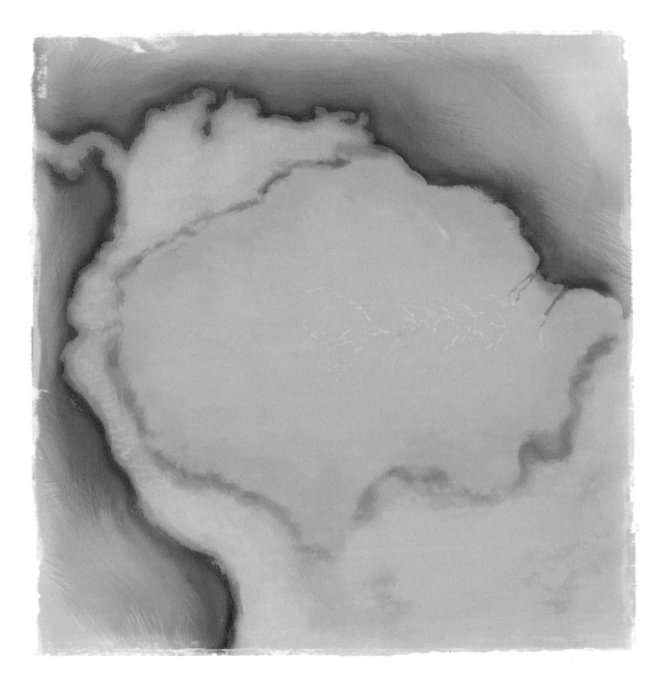

"Yes, you can!" said the toucan,

echoing deep in the amazon jungle.

"Yes, you can!" said the
toucan, yet again.

"You can do anything you put your mind to, as long as you believe in yourself!" explained Mother Toucan to her little toucans as they gathered around.

"But we're scared to fly!"
the little toucans all replied.

"Don't let your fears hold you back!"
Mother Toucan continued.

"When you push through
your fears, you will prove
to yourself that you can do
some pretty amazing
things!"

"Flying is fun! Especially when you learn how to do really cool tricks!"
she exclaimed.

"And you know what the best part about flying is?

One gets to explore and see the WORLD!"
she said, even more excitedly.

"You get to visit places
like ... China!

"... Paris!"

"... And New York City!"
she added, joyously.

The little toucans' eyes grew wide and bright.
They were in awe of their mother's tale.

"I was scared too," she continued.
"But I pushed through being scared
and decided I wanted to explore
and travel the world, and so I did."

The little toucans looked at each other,
awaiting what Mother Toucan
was about to say next.

"And now, it's your turn …
Try it!" Mother Toucan
exclaimed.

It was now the moment of truth.
The little toucans gathered,
carefully looking over the edge,
as they gauged the great, big plunge.

Their faces were stunned and
filled with fear.

And then, suddenly— "Eeeek!"

ONE TAKES THE LEAP!

"WOO WHOO!"
Exclaimed the little flying
toucan, as she gracefully
soared across the sky.

"Com'on guys! This is FUN!"
She joyfully shouted as
she encouraged her
siblings to join her.

By now, the remaining
little toucans built up the
courage to take the leap
and quickly joined their
sister in on the fun.

And Mother Toucan ...
she joined in on the fun too!

"Mom ... like you, do you
think we all can explore
and travel the world too?"
one of the little toucans asked.

"Yes, you can ..."
Mother Toucan replied sweetly.
"Yes, you can."

And as they joyously
drifted into the sunset,
she added "Where do you
want to go next?"

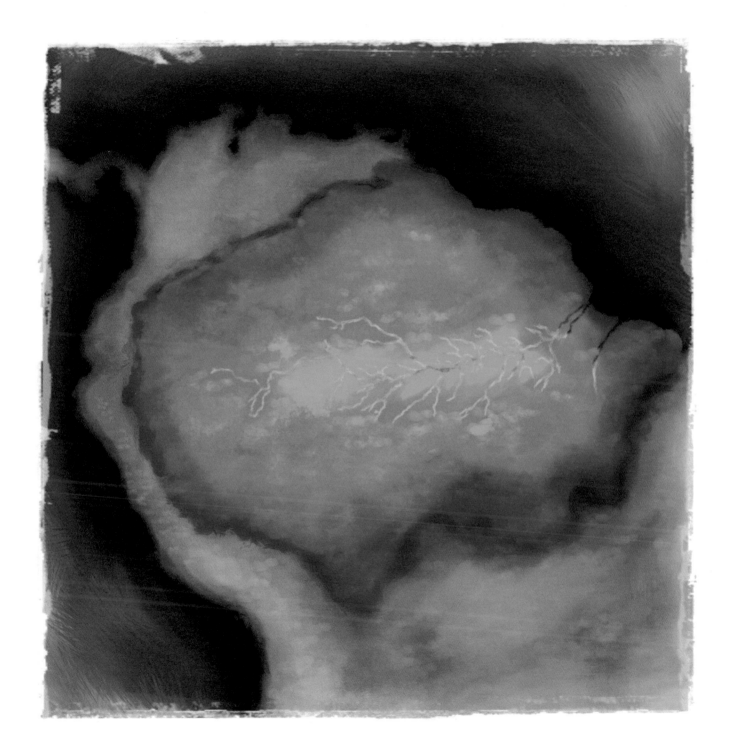

... Adventure awaits!

ABOUT THE AUTHOR

After going through a career change and finding herself in need of a creative outlet, Mariana created and wrote "Yes, You Can! Said the Toucan" as a direct message to her inner child in conquering one's fears. She felt the need to share this message with young readers to positively influence them in their own moments of fear and uncertainty. "Yes, You Can! Said the Toucan" is the first in a potential series of books designed to encourage young readers with excitement and teach them important, yet simple, life values and principles.

Originally from Venezuela, Mariana migrated to South Florida with her family at the age of eight. Mariana currently resides in Los Angeles, California.

Made in the USA
Las Vegas, NV
13 February 2022

43891258R00026